THE TREASURE OF CRAZY HORSE

TERRY DEARY

ILLUSTRATED BY JOHN EASTWOOD

A & C BLACK • LOND[O]

Black Cats

The Ramsbottom Rumble • Georgia Byng
Calamity Kate • Terry Deary
Ghost Town • Terry Deary
The Custard Kid • Terry Deary
The Treasure of Crazy Horse • Terry Deary
Dear Ms • Joan Poulson
It's a Tough Life • Jeremy Strong
Big Iggy • Kaye Umansky

First paperback edition 2001
First published in hardback 1990 by
A & C Black (Publishers) Ltd
37 Soho Square, London W1D 3QZ

ISBN 0-7136-5995-5

A CIP catalogue for this book is available from the
British Library.

Printed and bound in Spain by G. Z. Printek, Bilbao.

The Cactus Kid

My name is Cactus . . . the Cactus Kid, they call me round these parts. And I'm the toughest cowboy in the Wild, Wild West.

Just like my old Dad. Why, he was so tough, he used to chew the heads off rattlesnakes, just for fun. Then, one day, he chewed the wrong end: the angry snake turned round and bit him.

Poor old Dad!

So Ma was left to bring me up. She worked sixteen hours a day as the town blacksmith. In her spare time, she made a few extra dollars at the Dirty Shame Saloon. She would wrestle grizzly bears to entertain the customers. Ma was tough too. One night, she was beating the hide off an old grizzly when the bear cheated: it drew a gun and shot her.

Poor old Ma!

So I became an orphan at the tender age of ten. I grew up tough and I grew up angry. I had the prickliest temper in town: that's why they used to call me Cactus. And the name sort of stuck . . . like one of Ma's flap-jacks in the pan. She never could cook. Poor old Ma!

I learned to draw a gun faster than the beat of a

bluebird's wing, to shoot straighter than a sun-beam, and to stick to the back of a horse tighter than a flea with teeth. By the time I was thirteen, I was feared in Sad Gulch Town more than a black-widow spider.

No one ever bothered the Cactus Kid. Not until I met that pesky girl. Let me tell you about her.

As I recall, it all began around high noon in the bar-room of the Dirty Shame Saloon...

Sally Starr

I was playing poker. A skinny little bar-room girl was dealing out the cards. She whirled those cards like a Texas tornado – and sucked up my money just about as fast. I'd lost ninety dollars already, and she just sat there grinning.

Her name was Sally Starr. Her ugly little face was a mass of freckles, her short hair was like bleached straw and her nose was thin enough to cut cheese . . .

Don't believe a word the Cactus Kid tells you! I'm a pretty girl with hair like gold – and most people think my freckles are kind of cute. Perhaps my nose is a little on the fine side. But you ought to see that lump of dough in the middle of the Cactus Kid's clown-face! Yeuch!

Sally

Sorry, friends, I forgot to tell you. Sally says this is her story as much as mine, so she plans to stick in her skinny nose – er, sorry, her *fine* nose – whenever she thinks I've got the story wrong.

Anyway, there I was, playing cards with Sally and losing every cent I'd ever saved. At that moment, she looked about as cute as a poke in the eye with a bent stick.

'Put your money down, cowboy,' she said.

'I haven't any left!' I snapped in my prickliest tone. 'All I have left in the world is my gun and my horse.'

'I'll play you for them,' she said with a greedy gleam in her beady green eye – and her beady *blue* eye was gleaming too, on the other side of her nose.

Now Cactus is being just plain silly. I have a perfect, matching pair of cornflower blue eyes. Sally

I didn't know if I should gamble with my horse or not. I couldn't decide.

'What's your horse worth?' she asked suddenly.

'Twenty-five . . . thirty dollars,' I said with a shrug.

'Tell you what: we'll cut the cards,' she said. 'The highest card wins. If I win, I get the horse. But if *you* win I'll pay you four times what the horse is worth!'

'One hundred dollars!' I gasped.

'One hundred dollars,' she nodded.

'I don't know . . .'

'Take it. It's a great offer,' said the cowboy on my right. Misery Mike, his name was. So I nodded to Sally Starr.

'You cut first,' the girl said.

I licked my lips. I was scared. All or nothing on the turn of a card.

I lifted the top half of the pack and turned it. 'King of Diamonds!' cried Misery Mike. 'Only an ace could beat that!'

Even Sally managed a small smile. 'Looks like I owe you a hundred dollars, cowboy,' she said. Sally gathered a pile of dollars and began to push them across the table. I reached out to take them.

'Just a moment!' she said with a wicked glint in her *cornflower* blue eyes. 'I may as well cut the cards...just to *prove* that I'd never draw an ace.' She slipped her small hand over the pack and turned a card.

'Ace of Spades!' Misery Mike called. 'Sally Starr wins your horse! She drew the death card!'

Death! That's what I felt like as I turned away from that card table.

'Oh, Cactus!' Sally called after me.

I swung round. She threw a silver dollar on the table. 'Buy yourself a few drinks with that: drown your sorrows!'

I'd rather have drowned *her*! But I had to look like a good loser. I stumbled over to the bar and threw my last coin on it. 'Four shots of red-eye!' I ordered. The barman poured them.

I took the drinks to a corner table.

That was the most important move I ever made in my life.

3

The Indian Map

Two Indians sat at the table next to mine. They were arguing loudly, but no one took any notice. No one even understood. You see, they were talking the Flatfoot Indian language. But I'd been to school with a Flatfoot Indian girl and I'd picked up some of their words.

'Crazy Horse...' the fat one was saying. 'Treasure...'

I sat up. Treasure! I could do with some of that myself.

'Liar!' spat the little Indian with the face of a vulture.

The fat Indian jumped angrily to his feet. He struggled with something tucked inside his hat. At last he pulled out a piece of parchment, '...map!' he said, and spread it on the table.

I was itching to steal a closer look at that map, but the Indians were huddled over it. '... Ghost Town...' I heard the thin one mutter. 'But *where?*'

'Well, well, well!' the fat one chuckled, this time in English.

I was puzzled, but the thin one seemed to understand. At that moment, I knew I had to get my hands on that map. And the thin Indian seemed to have had the same idea. For the next hour, he kept his partner's glass filled with whisky. Slowly, the fat Indian's head began to sink, until it came to rest on the table. His fat little hat slipped off his fat little head.

His thin friend slipped a skinny, vulture claw into the hat and slid the yellowed paper inside his own buckskin jacket. Quickly he crept towards the saloon door and out into the afternoon sun.

Just as quickly, I moved after him!

As I hurried round to the stables to pick up my quarter horse, the Indian was climbing on to a piebald pony. I knew I'd catch him easily.

'Give me my horse: the bay mare!' I said to the stable-boy. He started to untie her.

'Stop!' came a voice from the shadows. It was a voice about as pretty as a jack-ass with a sore throat. It was Miss Sally Starr. 'That horse belongs to me,' she said. 'Cactus lost it in one of our card games.'

'You keep out of this, Needle-nose!' I yelled.

'Call me all the names you like...They don't change the fact the horse was won fair and square. You touch it, and I'll call the sheriff!' the freckle-faced tabby cat cried.

'Look, there's a fortune in gold riding down that road. If I had a horse to chase it, I'd pay you *ten times* what you won in that game!'

'Cut the cackle and quit the cow-shed, Cactus,' said Sally.

That sort of stupid remark doesn't deserve a reply – so I didn't make one.

To tell the truth, he was too dumb to think of a reply to my sharp wit. Sally

I snatched up my saddle-bag and water bottle, and walked out. I'd find that Indian even if I had to *walk* all the way to Ghost Town!

But by sundown, I'd only covered twenty miles. I'd reached the Bacon Tree Rocks. My feet were so swollen that I couldn't get my boots off. I just unrolled my blanket and lay down on the stony ground.

Funny name, I thought, as I drifted off to sleep.

Bacon is ham.

Tree is bush.

Bacon Tree... Ham Bush.

Hambush.

Ambush!

I sat up suddenly. In the bright moonlight, I saw a head bob up behind some rocks. A head too fair to be Indian – but a movement too careful to be anyone up to any good.

I could fight... or I could run...

4

The Ambush

I decided to fight on the run.

For a few moments, the fair head dropped behind the cover of a boulder. I took the chance to snatch my blanket and push it into my saddle-bag. Picking up my water bottle, I ran for the shadow of a rocky overhang.

I tugged my gun from its holster. My eyes were growing used to the frost-blue light of the moon. So, when the head bobbed up again, I was ready.

Maybe I was nervous. Anyway, I snapped off my shot too quickly . . . and missed.

I was upset at wasting one of my six, precious bullets. Five left now.

The bullet went singing off a Bacon Tree boulder – but the echoes were drowned by a scream!

Then a voice wailed. 'Don't shoot! Don't shoot, you bean-brained, skunk-scented cow-catcher!'

I sighed. 'Come on out, Freckles!'

And Sally Starr stepped into the space between two boulders. She'd changed her satin bar-room gown for checked shirt, jeans and a leather jacket.

'What are *you* doing here?' I asked.

'Put that gun away and I'll tell you,' she snapped.

I slid the gun back into its holster.

She walked across to me. 'I'm following you,' she said simply.

'Why?'

'Because you said you were going after a fortune in gold . . . Thought I'd see if you needed any help.' Without her fancy bar-room clothes, she looked almost pretty – and much younger. If I wasn't the toughest cowboy in the Wild, Wild West, I might even have felt a little sorry for her. Instead I said, 'Why would *you* need a fortune in gold? You were on your way to winning one with those card games back in the Dirty Shame Saloon.'

She shrugged shyly. 'Well, just after you left, one of the cowboys spotted how I was cheating. They made me give back the money and they gave me half an hour to get out of town . . .'

'Cheating! You mean I lost my horse and all my savings because you *cheated*?' My famous prickly temper was just about to blow my head off.

'Sorry, Cactus . . . But a girl has to make a living. Especially when she's a poor orphan . . .'

'So am I. And I've been a lot *more* poor since I met you,' I snarled.

'Take me with you,' she said with a small smile. It was enough to make even the toughest cowboy soften up just a little.

'Why should I take you with me? What good would it do me?'

'I'm a great tracker! Dad was a scout with the Seventh Cavalry, and he taught me all he knew. I can follow any trail, day or night. I even followed yours to find you here,' she said, to prove it. 'Now that your Indian friend is heading into rocky country, only a real expert could stick to his trail!'

That was true.

The trail *was* getting fainter and I *was* worried about picking it up the next morning. 'I'll give you a try. But if you lose the trail, then you go!'

Sally grinned. 'That's a deal.'

She dumped herself on the ground. 'You don't mind if I take your blanket, do you?' she asked, taking it from my saddle-bag. And before I could argue, she was wrapped in it and slipping off to sleep.

I was going to be cold that night. Just as well I'm tough.

He's about as tough as butter in the noon-day sun! Under all that prickly temper and tough talk, he's really quite sweet . . . And he was a real gentleman, letting me borrow that old blanket. Sally

I could bear the cold . . . and the stones digging into my back. What kept me awake that night was worry. Worry about whether I was doing the right thing in taking this skinny kid with me.

Of course he was doing the right thing. In fact, it was the best thing he'd ever done in his life. Not only am I charming and good company on a journey, but I'm pretty smart too – as you will see. Sally

5

Indian Trail

By noon the next day, we'd found the Indian's trail again.

What he means is that I'd found the Indian's trail. Cactus couldn't find water if you dropped him in a lake!

Sally

As we reached the edge of the Parcho Desert, the grass faded from green to brown. The ground was as dry as one of my old Ma's cakes – poor old Ma, never could cook – and soon even the cactuses were panting for a drink. Then Sally gave a cry.

'What's wrong?' I asked. 'Stepped on a cactus?'

'No. The only cactus I'd like to step on is you!' she snapped. 'Look at the ground and you'll see what's strange.'

I looked.

I looked again.

'Er . . . dusty, isn't it?' I said feebly.

'No more dusty than your brain!' she sneered. 'I mean look at the trail!'

I must have looked blank because she went on to explain: 'The hoof prints of the pony go off into the East – but this set of footprints goes straight ahead into the desert.'

'So, the Indian decided it would be quicker to walk,' I shrugged.

'Hmm. Unlikely. And look! See that big dent in the ground?' It was a hollow about the size of two dinner plates. Sally crouched near the spot and touched it. 'Damp,' she murmured. 'And a trail of dampness alongside the footprints – now we have a real chance of catching that Indian.'

'But why?' I asked. 'What do those signs mean?'

'Don't you know?' she smiled. She looked so smug that I could have buried her in the sand up to her neck. Well, could *you* guess?

Sally folded her arms and grinned at me. 'Over in England they say there's a famous detective called Sherlock Holmes...Cleverest man in the world...*He* could work it out.'

My cactus prickles were bristling. 'As clever as you, is he?' I snarled.

'Yes...but not so pretty.'

'So, tell me what you think the signs mean, Sherlock Starr.'

'It's easy,' she said. (She *would* say that.) 'That dent shows the Indian hit the ground pretty hard: he must have fallen off his pony. The pony ran off to the East because it had more sense than to go into the desert. The Indian got to his feet and started walking straight ahead – the shortest way to Ghost Town.'

I nodded. It made sense so far. 'So he's walking

across the desert?' I muttered and looked through the shimmering heat haze across the baking sands. 'Hope he has plenty of water.'

'He hasn't!' Sally said gleefully. 'That trail of dampness must be a leaking water bottle! He must have cracked the bottle when he fell.'

And, sure enough, we found the cracked, empty water bottle a mile further on. 'He's thrown it away!' Sally purred, pleased as a cat with a bucket of cream.

I nodded. 'If he'd had any sense, he'd have turned back by now. He wouldn't head into the desert without water. He must be crazy!'

'Or crazy with the greed for gold. Some people will do anything for gold,' Sally said.

'Yeah! Even cheat at cards!' I growled.

Sally pulled a pained face. She looked so miserable, I almost felt sorry for her. I changed the subject. 'You really think he'd go on without water?'

She frowned and shook her head. 'That map must show a water-hole,' she said slowly.

Of course she guessed right. Just lucky, I suppose.

Not lucky – just cleverer than Cactus!

Sally

The first sign of the Indian was the circle of vultures in the sky...waiting. Ten minutes later, we saw the man himself. He was on his hands and knees, trying to crawl away from the water-hole. He looked weak and ill.

'Umbah . . . water,' he managed to gasp.

'You want "umbah"? You want water?' I asked.

He shook his head and pointed towards the still, green water. '*Umbah* water!' he repeated.

'Oh, I see! You call the water-hole Umbah Water?' He nodded and made a sudden grab for the bottle at my belt. I stepped back quickly.

'Not so fast. We'll do a deal. You give me that map in your pocket, and I'll give you enough water to get you back to town.'

The Indian panted painfully for a few minutes, shaking his head and moaning. At last he slowly pulled the yellowed paper from his pocket. I snatched it from him and hid it inside my shirt.

When he'd drunk enough, I helped him to his feet. 'This gun is loaded,' I said, patting my holster. 'You try to follow me, and I'll fill you so full of holes that the water you've had will all leak out!'

But I didn't need threats. 'Enough!' he grunted, and then slouched back along his trail of footprints. Back to the town of Sad Gulch.

I opened the map, excited. 'Here we are . . . Umbah Water,' I said, pointing out the spot to Sally. 'Let's just fill up our water bottles from here. There's still some desert to cross and we don't want to run out.'

But, of course, Sherlock Smarty-pants Starr had other ideas.

6

The Parcho Desert

Sally snatched the water bottle from my grasp. 'Wait!' she cried. 'I'm not so sure that's a good idea. What does "umbah" mean?'

'I don't know *exactly*,' I admitted. 'The Flatfoot girl I knew at school used to call me "umbah boy"...I suppose it must mean "sweet" or "good".'

Of course, Cactus would suppose that.

Sally

'Hmm!' Sally nodded. 'I think we should take a chance and cross the last ten miles just with the water we still have left from town.'

She pushed aside the green scum at the edge of Umbah Water, and looked down into the brown murk beneath. She dipped a finger in and licked it. 'Yeuch!' Her face screwed up so that all her freckles were squashed into one mass – a bit like a treacle pudding only not so sweet.

'Salt water! No wonder that Indian was crawling *away* from the water when we met him! Didn't you spot that, Cactus?' She was using her I-told-you-so voice. 'Just as well I told you not to fill the bottle here!'

And of course I had told him so! I'd saved the clown's life! He just doesn't like to admit that I'm smarter than him. Sally

I tried to remember my school days. Suddenly it all came back to me. The little Indian girl had had a long plait of hair down her back. I'd just been given a new hunting knife for my eighth birthday: Ma had made it herself in her blacksmith's shop. I was ever so proud of it. I wanted to try it out – so I cut off the Indian girl's plait. She turned round to me and screamed, 'Umbah Boy!' Perhaps 'umbah' didn't mean sweet, after all...Perhaps it meant nasty or rotten! Sally was right again, and I was cross.

'Let's get moving,' I sighed, 'before you cut your mouth with that sharp little tongue.'

Sally just laughed.

We didn't argue much after that. Talking made our mouths dry, so we trudged in silence for the next three or four hours. Our water bottle was finally empty, but at least the evening was cooler.

At last we reached a small stream running into the mouth of a small canyon: the map called it Bandit Canyon. I threw myself on the ground and filled myself to the brim with cool fresh water. So did Sally, but then she began inspecting the mud at the edge of the stream.

'What can you see?' I asked.

'Hoof prints,' she said quietly and looked over her shoulder. 'I can make out the prints of at least three different horses.'

'Great! Wild horses!' I cried. 'If we can catch a couple, we'll get a ride to Ghost Town!'

'But the marks of these hoof prints show . . .'

I cut Sally off. There was no time to waste arguing. Soon it would be too dark to catch anything. Even I could see that the hoof prints led into the right fork of the canyon . . . and the map showed that that was a dead end. The horses would be trapped. Easy!

Still, Sally had to argue. She wanted to take the left hand fork – *away* from the prints. I have to admit she's usually right . . . But she couldn't be right all the time, could she?

Couldn't I? Sally

Perhaps I *should* have listened to her.

7

Bandit Canyon

The canyon was cool and shady as the sun sank in a purple sky. Still, the trail was easy to follow.

'But *Cactus*!' Sally moaned. 'Can't you see the marks of the horses' shoes?'

'Of course I can . . . and I'm following them!' I snapped.

'But we're looking for *wild* horses . . . and the horses that made those tracks *aren't* wild!'

'Look, Sherlock Sal,' I sighed, 'I *know* you're good at tracking – but even you can't tell how wild a horse is, just by looking at its hoof prints!'

Sally grabbed my arm fiercely. 'Of course I can, stupid! I asked if you could see the marks of their shoes and you said yes. Well, wild horses don't *have* shoes. Only tame horses have shoes put on by a blacksmith.'

'Ah . . . of course . . . I know that!' I stammered.

He didn't. Sally

'I was just thinking, er, those could be tame horses that have escaped!' I said lamely.

Sally shook her head and gave me a look of pity. 'Those horses belong to someone – and the only sort of someone who'd live in a wild place like this would be a bandit-someone.'

'I'm not scared of bandits,' I scoffed.

'You should be,' came a soft, deep voice. I looked up sharply. A man with a dirty, yellow beard and matching teeth was grinning at us. His left hand held a gun; his right hand held nothing. Because he had no right hand. His empty shirt sleeve flapped in the evening breeze.

'Are you a bandit?' Sally gasped.

'That's right.'

'But you only have one arm,' I argued.

'Sure,' he frowned. 'You never heard of a one-armed bandit?'

'Are you scared?' Sally whispered to me.

'No,' I said. 'You can see he's quite armless!'

Then I heard two metallic clicks behind me, and swung round to see two more one-armed bandits pointing ugly guns at us. 'We don't like that kind of joke, stranger,' snarled the red-bearded one.

'That's right,' agreed his black-bearded partner. 'If one more smart-alec cowboy tells me to go to a second-hand shop, then I'll scream!'

Sally stepped in front of me and said firmly. 'Take no notice of Cactus here. He likes to talk tough, but he doesn't mean any arm...Sorry! Harm! *Harm*! I meant to say HARM!'

Ugly Yellow-beard looked even uglier. 'Enough of this wise-cracking. Back to business, Cactus. Your money or your wife!'

'Well, I haven't any money, and this young lady isn't my wife,' I said.

'Shall I shoot him now, Lefty?' Red-beard asked.

'But we *do* have a treasure map!' Sally cried quickly.

'Hand it over, stranger,' Black-beard ordered.

I hadn't come all that way just to hand over my map without a fight. 'No,' I said quietly.

Yellow-beard lowered his gun. To my surprise, he grinned. 'So you really are tough?'

'Tougher than you think,' I replied.

'Right, then you won't mind fighting for that map!'

He was big and strong...but he had only one arm. I reckoned I ought to be able to beat him.

'Take him now, Cactus,' Sally urged. The trouble was, I didn't trust his villainous friends to play fair and keep out of it. I hesitated.

'You don't scare me, you yellow-bearded, yellow-livered coyote!' I snarled.

The bandit's beard bristled with anger. 'Listen, kid, sticks and stones may break my bones – but calling me names will just get you a broken neck!'

'Oh yeah?' I said, backing away.

'Oh yeah!' he growled. Then he added, 'Grab him boys!' Suddenly I felt rough hands reach out to grab my shoulders. 'To the pit with him!' Yellow-beard cried.

I told him he should have fought. Sally

(If she says 'I told you so' once more, I swear her pointy nose will be pointing backwards!)

So there I was, being dragged to the pit by these villainous vermin.

'Not the pit!' Sally sobbed. 'You can't make poor Cactus dig for coal. He has very soft hands, you know!'

'What's she on about?' Red-beard asked.

'I don't know,' shrugged Black-beard. 'I think she's some kind of nut.' He turned to Sally. 'Listen, young lady, we aren't going to put your friend down a *coal* pit: we're putting him into a pit of rattlesnakes!'

'Oh, that's all right then!' Sally said.

'Is it?' I gasped.

'Is it?' the bandits echoed.

'Oh, yes! Cactus can bite the heads off rattlers.'

'Great! I've *got* to see this!' Black-beard cried.

'That's my *Dad* you're thinking of!' I wailed. '*I* couldn't bite the head off a tadpole!'

'Let's throw him in anyway, just for fun,' chuckled Red-beard.

So I was dragged, struggling, to a deep hole in the floor of the canyon and thrown in. Flaming torches lit the steep, rocky sides of the pit and showed that there was no way out. Then I heard a soft hissing behind me. I spun round, drew my gun and fired. That was when I realised the bandits had at least left me my gun.

The scared snake slithered back into its rocky hollow. A second snake came from my right; I spun and fired. If that snake had had hair, then my bullet would have parted it.

A third snake took a bullet clean through its rattle.

The next one had a fang shot out, then slid away to safety.

There was just one snake left to deal with.

I fired . . . and missed.

'Give in, Cactus?' Black-beard jeered from above. 'Will you come out and fight now?' he asked.

I looked at that last evil rattler. Its little yellow eyes glinted in the torch-light. A forked tongue flickered over its bloodless lips. I could try and shoot it again . . . and now it was so close that I knew I couldn't miss.

The trouble was that I wasn't sure if I still had a bullet left in my gun.

I'd left Sad Gulch Town with six bullets. Had I used them all?

I had two seconds to decide whether to shoot – or agree to fight.

8

Fist Fight in Bandit Canyon

'OK!' I called to Yellow-beard. 'I'll fight you!'

The bandit dropped a rope down the pit. I grabbed it and scrambled up. The angry snake, cheated of its prey, hissed and rattled at me.

I panted on the top edge of the pit and caught my breath.

'Why did you change your mind?' Sally asked. 'You only fired five shots. You could have killed that last snake and been free.'

And for once, Miss Smarty-pants was wrong! I laughed. 'I fired five shots, but that's all I had. You forget that I used one shooting at you last night. My gun was empty!'

I felt pleased with myself and knew I could beat the bandit. I needed just a little time to finish the plan that was forming in my mind.

'First let me have a drop of water and a bite to eat. I've had a hard day's walking.'

'Sure,' said Red-beard, putting his gun away and wrapping his one arm around my shoulder. 'Come back to the camp and we'll feed you.'

'Great!' Sally cried, 'I'm starving.'

'Oh, you'll find we live well here – all the wild-life we can eat. Why, we can offer you a choice of skunk steaks, porcupine pies, rattlesnake rolls or mouse mousse!'

'Actually, I'm not very hungry at all,' Sally said weakly.

Yellow-beard shrugged. 'In that case, let's get on with the fight.'

'Suits me,' I said. My plan was ready. 'If I win, I go free.'

'*We* go free!' Sally put in quickly. I couldn't really leave her with the bandits, could I?

I told you he was a gentleman, didn't I? Sally

'And if *I* win I get the treasure map?' said Yellow-beard.

'And your friends stay out of this, whatever happens?'

'Suits us,' the other two grinned.

'Then I agree,' I said. 'Let's shake on it.'

'Shake what?' he asked.

'Shake hands!' I said.

'But I've only got one,' Yellow-beard croaked sadly.

'That'll do,' I told him. I reached out and took his left hand in mine. We shook hands...but I didn't let go. The bandit's right sleeve flapped uselessly; my right sleeve was full of arm. I stretched that arm up and pulled his beard.

'Ouch!' he yelled. 'Let go of my hand!'

'Nothing in the rules that says I have to,' I grinned. Then I pulled his beard again.

'Ah-oooh!' wailed Yellow-beard. 'This isn't fair!' He struggled to free his arm but I held on tight. Then I twisted his nose.

'Yeee-ahhh!' he cried and his eyes began to water.

'Give in?' I asked.

'No-o!'

I poked him in the eye. 'Give in?'

'Well...maybe!'

I took a firm grip on his beard again. 'Give in?'

'Don't pull my beard, please! All right, all right, all right! I give in!'

I released him and let him fall to the ground, rubbing his chin and sobbing.

'In that case, we'll be on our way,' I said, and gripped Sally quickly by the elbow.

'But you can't go!' Black-beard cried.

I was afraid I wouldn't get away with just that struggle with Yellow-beard. I'd have to take on the other two – and they wouldn't be falling for any hand-shake tricks.

Sally stepped forward angrily. 'Look, you hairy half-wits, you promised we could go free if we beat Lefty. So keep your promise!'

'But we never let anyone leave Bandit Canyon . . . not until we've treated them to a party!' Red-beard said in a hurt voice.

'A party?' Sally said.

'Sure! Food, drink and a song or two!' Yellow-beard said eagerly, rising to his feet with a friendly grin.

Sally and I looked at one another. We shrugged. 'Sure. Why not?'

So we watched the sun set over the plains, as we chewed on fried leg of lizard and sang cowboy songs. We stamped our feet and clapped our hands. At least, Sally and I clapped our hands; the one-armed bandits just stamped their feet, of course.

By the time the midnight moon rose the bandits were snoring loudly. I borrowed a handful of bul-lets from Black-beard's gun belt, then Sally and I crept away. By the light of the pale moon I read the map.

'Where to now, Cactus?' Sally whispered.

'Back to the fork at the mouth of the canyon . . . We should have turned left,' I said.

'I told you . . .' she began and then she saw the anger in my eyes.

The truth is, I remembered how Cactus had fought for my freedom. Just this once, I let him off.
Sally

So we slipped through the shadows of the deep canyon and shuddered as the coyotes howled like hungry wolves. Sally was so scared that she gripped hard on to my arm.

If you must know I was just a little cold.
Sally

'Where are we going to sleep?' she asked.

'There are some caves in the side wall of the canyon,' I explained and pointed to black shadows on the moon-silver slopes. 'We can rest there and go on in the morning.'

We crawled into the nearest cave, lay on the soft sand floor and closed our eyes happily; we soon dropped off. Off into sweet-dreamed sleep.

Perhaps, if we'd known what was in those caves, we'd have had nightmares.

9

The Caves of the Flatfoot

The sun woke us early on the third day of our journey. Sally grinned. 'Pass the map, Cactus,' she said. 'I'll have a look and see how much further it is to Ghost Town.'

Early in the morning I'm at my prickliest. I just grunted and pushed the map at her. Sally unfolded it. She followed our route with her finger. Suddenly she gasped and turned whiter than her bleached hair. 'Cactus!' she whispered. 'These caves ... They're marked on here as Flatfoot Indian caves.'

'So?'

'So they're Flatfoot *burial* caves!'

'Let me see!' I snatched the map back and glanced at it. 'You're right.'

Sally rolled up the blanket quickly. 'Let's get out of this cave at once. We'll head back towards the Parcho Desert and round to the Flatto Plateau.'

I studied the map carefully. 'That's a long way round,' I said. 'Could add a whole day to the journey. If you look carefully at the map, you can see there's a path through the caves that would lead us straight on to the Lonesome Prairie and...'

'Go *into* the burial caves!' Sally screeched. 'We might get got by ghosts!'

'You're safe with me,' I told her.

'Oh yeah?' she sniffed.

'Don't you trust me?' I asked. 'Me, the toughest cowboy in the Wild, Wild West?'

'No,' Sally said shortly.

Well, would you trust Cactus to protect you against a ghost? Sally

'I still say we could save time by cutting through the caves,' I argued. 'If there are any Flatfoot Indians in there then they're dead and buried. They can't hurt us.'

'If you're sure,' Sally moaned, and we headed into the clammy, cold cave. The walls were slimy and gave off a greeny glow that helped to light our way. The tunnel twisted and forked like a maze. We could only guess the right path.

'Don't be scared,' I said after half an hour.

'I'm not scared, now we're in here. I'm quite enjoying it,' Sally said.

'Then why are your teeth chattering?'

'My teeth aren't chattering,' she said. 'I thought *yours* were!'

'Well, *something's* rattling!' I snapped, losing my prickly temper.

'Sorry,' said a hollow voice behind us. 'My bones do tend to rattle when I walk.'

I turned cold. Then I turned round. A tall skeleton grinned at me. I suppose he had to grin at me, since he had no lips to cover his teeth. 'You must be one of the Indians buried here,' I said weakly.

'That's right,' he said. 'But how can you tell that I'm an Indian?'

'You still have a feather stuck in your skull,' Sally pointed out.

'So I have!' cried the skeleton, and he gave a rattling laugh. 'Anyway, I just rose from my grave to warn you that you're going the wrong way.'

'We are?' I gasped.

'Oh yes! At this rate, you'll end up like me! You'd never unlock the secret of these twisting paths.'

'Don't tell us: to unlock them, we'd need a skeleton key,' Sally giggled.

'Will you get us out of here?' I asked.

The skeleton sighed. 'I suppose so. The trouble is that I need a lot of spirit energy to move this skeleton. I quickly become tired...'

'He's just bone idle,' I whispered to Sally.

Sally shivered. 'Can we get on, then? I'm chilled to the marrow.'

'Oh! You needn't complain – your marrows are better covered than mine.' The skeleton turned and moved with jerky steps along the rock-floored corridor. 'Follow me, pale-faces.'

In the green glow, we followed him as he jigged along the paths that wound like a corkscrew through the rock. All the time, the skeleton chatted about life – I mean *death* – in the caves, and told the tragic tales of the Indians buried there.

'Where are their skeletons, then?' I asked.

'Resting. Their spirits are at peace in the Happy Hunting Grounds.'

'Then why isn't yours?' I asked again.

'I was buried without my treasure,' he groaned. 'I can never rest until that treasure is buried along with my bones. Until it is, then I'm doomed to wander these caves alone.'

We didn't ask too many more questions after that. The ghost-skeleton seemed lost in his gloomy thoughts.

*Perhaps we should have asked more questions –
shown more interest in the ghost's grim tale. But we were
selfish: too worried by our own problems to think about
anyone else's. It could have saved us a lot of trouble,
later.*

Sally

Within half an hour, we could smell fresh,
grass-scented air, and five minutes later we stepped out into the sunlight of the Lonesome Prairie.

'Goodbye, Cactus and Sally,' the ghost-
skeleton said with a wave of his hand bones.

'Goodbye...er...Sorry, we don't know your
name,' Sally said.

'Ahh!' sighed the skeleton. 'When I was alive I
was called Crazy Horse.' Then he vanished back
into the caves.

10

The Lonesome Prairie

Sally and I looked at each other. 'The treasure of Crazy Horse,' Sally whispered.

'I wonder if he'd have helped us if he'd known that we were planning to steal his treasure?' I said.

That thought kept us quiet for the journey over the prairie. So did the sight of the endless green vastness – longer and wider than even the Parcho Desert.

Dust filled my mouth. It even covered Sally Starr's freckles, so it must have been thick!

If it filled the Cactus Kid's mouth, then it was the thickest dust in the world! Sally

A herd of a thousand buffalo grazed peacefully on the prairie. Sally whispered, 'Are they dangerous?'

I laughed. 'No chance. One shot from this gun and they'd be off across the prairie faster than a grass-fire in a gale!'

But I spoke a little too soon. One huge buffalo seemed to have fixed his eyes on us and began lumbering after us. I began to walk more quickly.

The buffalo began to trot.

We started to run.

The buffalo broke into a gallop.

'I thought you said they were harmless!' Sally cried as she stumbled through the thick grass.

I glanced over my shoulder. The buffalo was so close that I could see some kind of collar around his neck. I drew my gun and aimed dead between the eyes.

'No!' Sally screamed.

'It's him or us!' I shouted and pulled back the hammer on my gun.

'Don't shoot!' she yelled.

My finger trembled on the trigger but something made me stop.

I made him stop! Sally

I lowered the gun slowly. When the charging buffalo was just five paces from us, he dug in his front hooves and skidded to a stop. He lowered his shaggy head and gently nuzzled Sally.

Go on, Sally, say it.

'But how did you know he was harmless?' I asked her.

'Elementary, my dear Watson!'

'Watson? Who's he?'

'Sherlock Holmes's stupid friend?' she grinned.

'Well, my dear Holmes, how did you know?' I asked as I slipped my gun back into its holster.

'Wild buffalo don't have collars: this one must have escaped from a travelling circus. He knows human beings and that's why he came after us.'

I carefully took hold of the faded red collar round the buffalo's massive, woolly mane. The collar had once had gold words embroidered on it; I could still make out the words. '*William F. Cody's Wild West Show*,' I read aloud. 'Not a circus, then. William F. Cody . . . Hey, he's the famous Buffalo Bill!' And as I said the words, the animal seemed to nod its head.

'What would Buffalo Bill want with a tame buffalo?' Sally asked.

'Oh, his team of stunt riders would ride them in the shows,' I explained.

'Ride them!' Sally cried. 'Then perhaps we could ride this one over this prairie!'

I nodded slowly. 'It would certainly be quicker,' I agreed.

'Could you stay on his back without a saddle?' Sally asked.

'I can stick to a horse's back tighter than a flea with teeth!' I boasted. I leapt on to the animal's shoulder and hauled Sally up behind me. I gripped the buffalo's collar and nudged his sides with my heels. He moved off like a well-broken horse.

I reckon it would have taken us more than a day to walk across that Prairie. On the back of our buffalo, it took us just till the afternoon of that third day.

But even our tame buffalo couldn't help us over the next obstacle. We jumped down and I sent him back to join his herd. Then we stood and stared at the monster that lay in our path . . .

11

The Black River

I dipped a foot into the Black River that lay between us and Ghost Town. The water was bitterly cold and the current so strong that it almost sucked me in. I shook my head. 'No chance of swimming it,' I said.

'Let's walk along the edge and see if there's a crossing point higher up,' Sally suggested.

We set off up-river, looking for a place where it might become narrower and shallower. It was half an hour later that Sally spotted the old man. 'Look!' she cried. 'A ferry-man!'

'Ferry' was a rather grand name for the little rowing boat that sat on the near bank of the river. The old man lay dozing with a straw hat tilted over his face. A sign said: *Ferry – Five Dollars Each Way*.

'Hello, strangers!' the old man said, looking up. He gave us a charming smile. (At least, it *would* have been charming if he'd had any teeth.) 'Want to cross? That'll be ten dollars, please.'

'We don't have ten dollars,' I said.

'Then you don't cross the river,' he sniggered. That made my cactus-blood begin to boil.

'Five dollars is far too much,' I argued.

He just shrugged. 'I don't fix the price, mister.

The river marks the start of Flatfoot territory. *They tell me how much to charge.*'

My hand itched to pull my gun on him and just take the boat. But Sally stepped forward and said a stupid thing.

It wasn't at all stupid – it was part of my clever plan, as you'll see. Sally

She said, 'Anyway, I'll bet that shabby boat couldn't get us across the river without sinking.'

The old man's eyes glittered. 'Oh, you want to bet, do you? How much do you want to bet?'

'I'll bet you the Cactus Kid's gun – worth at least ten dollars,' Sally offered.

'My gun!' I gasped. 'Not my best Colt...'

'Quiet, Cactus,' she hissed from the corner of her mouth. 'I know what I'm doing.'

'It's a bet!' the old man said. 'If I get you across, then I get the gun?'

'On, no!' Sally said. 'What happens if you sink, like I reckon you will? We'd win the bet . . . but we'd lose the gun in the water anyway.'

'Hmm,' the old man muttered, stroking his bristly chin. 'See what you mean. Pity. I like a gamble.'

'I knew it as soon as I saw you,' Sally smiled – and winked quickly at me. 'Tell you what. Why don't we gamble with cards instead?'

'I don't have a pack of cards,' he moaned.

'Never mind: I just happen to have a pack here in my bag!' she said. 'We'll cut the cards – highest card wins. If you win you get the gun; if *we* win, then we get across free. OK?'

'A deal!' the old man chuckled. 'Haven't had so much fun since my wife got her tongue caught in the wash-tub mangle!'

He sucked at his pink gums, licked his fingers and cut the cards. 'Queen of Clubs!' he cried. 'That's going to take some beating!'

Sally sighed. 'It certainly is.' She reached for the pack of cards. I didn't dare to look. She cut them. 'My goodness!' she cried.

'You've lost,' I groaned. 'Don't tell me you've lost!'

'Would you believe it?' Sally gasped.

'I'd believe anything of you, you needle-nosed no-brain! You've lost us the gun *and* the chance to cross the river.'

'Oh no,' she said mildly. 'Look. King of Diamonds. I've won!'

The old man slapped his leg and chuckled. 'Never play cards with a woman, Daddy always told me... They have all the luck!'

What luck? Remember I told you they were my cards? My marked cards from the Dirty Shame Saloon. Of course I won: I cheated! Sally

The old man pushed the ferry into the fast-flowing river, and we jumped aboard. A lot of water seemed to be flowing *inside* the boat, but somehow we floundered across.

I staggered on to the far bank and began to breathe freely again. As the old man set off on the return journey, he called after us, 'Remember, you're now heading into Flatfoot Indian lands...'

12

The Nugget Mines

As we set off down the Ghost Town trail, the sun was getting lower in the sky. By evening, we'd reached an old rusting railway line that led to a black cavern in the hillside.

'The Nugget Mines,' I said, after checking the map. 'Let's go inside and shelter for the night.'

The air in the Nugget Mines was cool and stale. The last miners had left flints and torches, so we could light our way inside. We found tools scattered over the iron rails, lamps still half-full of oil and bowls half-full of rotting food. 'They must have left in a hurry,' Sally said softly.

'But why?' I asked. 'Why leave before you've even finished a plate of food?' Sally just shook her head. We stepped deeper into the gloomy tunnel – and found the answer to our puzzle. It was stuck firmly in a pit prop.

It was a Flatfoot arrow.

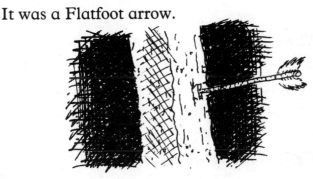

'They were attacked,' Sally said with a shudder. I nodded but didn't answer. I was too busy thinking of something else.

At last I spoke. 'Most people quit a mine when there's nothing left to dig for . . . but the men in this mine were still working . . . '

'So maybe there's still some gold in here!' Sally finished excitedly. We hurried forward to the end of the tunnel. There were several picks and shovels thrown into a part-filled truck of broken stones. And there, in the middle of the stone was a single, glistening nugget of gold.

'Not a fortune,' Sally said as she slipped it into her bag, 'but it may be useful.'

I let her take the gold. It was nothing to the fortune I'd have when we found Crazy Horse's treasure. Sally was looking at the fallen tools and the Flatfoot arrow. Even her freckles seemed to turn pale as she murmured, 'There are enough ghosts in here tonight. Let's sleep nearer the entrance.'

It was a fine warm evening, but as the sun set in the green-gold sky, Sally began to shiver. 'I'll light a fire,' I offered.

There was a lot of old wood around the mine entrance, and I soon had a steady blaze going. The smoke rose into the clear, still air. I found some dried beans and boiled them for us in a pan of water.

Some of the wood was damp and I had to fan it

with my blanket. The smoke rose into the sky in dark streaks. Suddenly, as we began to eat the beans, a deep voice said, 'Yes please.'

A tall Indian stood behind us. He held a tomahawk in one hand and a rifle in the other. My right hand crept towards my gun, but Sally stopped me.

'Yes please, what?' she asked.

'Yes please . . . I will share supper with you,' the Indian said. 'It was kind of you to ask.'

He sat down by the fire, crossing his long legs. As I served a plate of beans, I asked him carefully. 'Er, when did we ask you? I don't remember exactly.'

'Why, just now!' the Indian said. 'I read your smoke signal. "Come to supper," it said.'

'Ah – oh – yes! *That* smoke signal,' I said weakly.

The Indian finished his beans and grunted. 'Just as well you sent that signal,' he said. 'The Flatfoot have been watching you ever since you crossed the river into their lands.'

'They have?' I said nervously.

'Oh, yes. They were afraid you might be after the treasure of Crazy Horse!' he laughed.

And I laughed too. 'Ha ha ha! What an idea! As if we'd take Crazy Horse's treasure!'

Sally gave a scared giggle. 'We wouldn't do that!'

'Good,' the Indian snorted. 'The Flatfoot have searched for it for twenty years – but without the lost map, the search is hopeless.'

I clutched at the map inside my jacket and wondered what he'd do if he knew it was there. 'Why do the Flatfoot need the treasure?' I asked.

'It is not for the Flatfoot,' the Indian explained. 'That treasure must be found and buried with the bones of Crazy Horse. Until it is, the spirit of Crazy Horse will never be free to roam the Happy Hunting Grounds in the sky.'

Suddenly I felt sorry for the restless bones of Crazy Horse. The thought of his poor tired skeleton put me right off my boiled beans. He was such a friendly skeleton – and he had saved our lives. Sally

'But,' the Indian went on, 'your signal showed that you speak the Flatfoot language – and your offer of supper showed that you are friends. You may go your way in peace.' He slipped the tomahawk back into the belt of his buckskin suit. His dark eyes sparkled in the firelight and he seemed to look clean through me. 'If you ever find that you need the help of the Flatfoot, then give the cry of the owl three times: I, your friend, Blue Jay, will never be far away.'

'Thanks, Blue Jay – friend,' I grinned. But I wasn't too happy at the thought of him being so close when we reached the treasure. He picked up his gun and was gone as silently as a cat.

I gave a long sigh.

'I didn't know that you could do Flatfoot smoke signals,' Sally said, amazed.

'Neither did I,' I muttered. 'Let's get some sleep.'

Sally let me share my blanket that third night on the trail. I decided that perhaps she wasn't such a bad kid after all.

And I decided that Cactus wasn't such a bad kid, either. And it's about time somebody looked after the poor, motherless boy! Sally

As I drifted into sleep, I thought that with the Flatfoot on our side we *might* have a better chance of reaching Ghost Town tomorrow . . . Might . . .

13

The Fort Kearney Stage Coach

The next day, walking was easier. The road was clear and Sally was cheerful. Looking at the map, I reckoned we had just twenty miles to go. Apart from sore feet, it was more like a holiday than a treasure hunt.

Wandering happily down the middle of the dusty road almost got us killed. We were laughing and talking so much that we didn't hear the clattering of the hooves until they were almost at our backs. At the last moment, I turned and dragged Sally to one side. The Wells Fargo stage coach skidded to a halt a little way up the road.

'Where are you headed for?' Sally called up to the driver, a wrinkled old man. His young guard, who held a shot-gun and looked as nervous as a kitten in a kennel, seemed to think there was an Indian behind every rock or bush.

'We're going to Fort Kearney!' the driver shouted back.

'Do you pass through Ghost Town?' I asked.

The young guard gave a startled jump. 'G-g-ghost Town!' he gasped. 'We go ten miles out of our road to miss G-g-ghost Town!'

'What's wrong?' Sally jeered. 'Scared of the ghosts?'

'Nope! But we're afraid of the Flatfoot Indians,' the driver spat. 'You know that place ain't called Ghost Town because it's full of spooks. It's because it's deserted. And it's deserted because it's built on Flatfoot lands. When the Flatfoot found out about it, they came back and drove the settlers away. Only a fool would stop there now.'

'But how close can you drop us?' I asked.

'Oh, five miles from the town boundary, I guess,' he sniffed. 'If you can pay.'

'Money?' I said stupidly.

'Money – or gold,' he said.

Sally handed our nugget of gold to the stage driver. It seemed a pity to give all that just for a ten-mile ride. But the sun was getting hotter, my water bottle was getting emptier – and I'd soon have Crazy Horse's fabulous wealth anyway.

'Climb aboard!' the driver called. We climbed.

The cool shadows of the coach held only one passenger: an old lady in a black dress with a starched white collar. She sat as stiff as the rim of her black bonnet.

'Afternoon, ma'am,' I said politely. 'I'm the Cactus Kid and this here's my friend, Sally Starr. Hope you don't mind us joining you.'

'Nice to have some company,' she said with a cold smile. 'It's a long way to Fort Kearney.'

'Oh, but we're only going as far as Ghost Town,' Sally said excitedly. 'We're going to find Crazy Horse's treasure!'

The old lady's smile faded and her face hardened. 'Crazy Horse is dead. Better that he stays dead,' she snapped, frosty as an Alaskan moon.

'We weren't planning to dig him up – just find his treasure!' I pointed out.

'But Crazy Horse was an Indian war chief,' she said sternly. 'He led the Flatfoot into the Battle of Deadwood River. That's where the great General Rex Layton met a glorious death.'

'But the Flatfoot haven't been on the war path for ten years,' Sally argued.

'Only because they are poor and leaderless!' the old woman ranted. Pink spots of anger rose in her white cheeks. 'With Crazy Horse's treasure, they'd buy weapons; and they'd also view the finding of the treasure as a sign. A sign that they should fight again. And this time we haven't a great man like General Rex Layton to save us.' Her voice was hoarse and I thought she'd have a heart attack if I didn't calm her down.

'It's all right, ma'am. The Indians wouldn't have the treasure. *We* would!'

The old lady gave a sour twist to her thin, pale lips. 'Ghost Town is in the middle of the Flatfoot lands. You might get *in* to find the treasure . . . but you sure wouldn't get *out*. Leastways, not alive!'

'Ghost Town five miles ahead!' the old driver called back. 'This is as near as we go.'

Suddenly I wasn't so sure that I wanted to get off. But the coach pulled to a halt. I opened the door and helped Sally down. 'Good-bye,' the old lady said. 'And if you have any sense, you'll leave the treasure where it is and take the next stage back to Sad Gulch.'

'Good-bye, and thanks for the advice, Mrs er ... Mrs ...'

'Layton,' the old lady said. 'Mrs Rex Layton.' The coach pulled away with a jerk, and rattled off into the cool green hills.

A sign pointed down the dusty valley road: *Ghost Town – enter at your peril.* We set off to walk the longest five miles I've ever known.

14

Ghost Town

We were so near, and yet that road went on forever. I'd been on the trail four days so my feet were sore and my legs were aching. Walking was hard for me.

But talking wasn't hard for him. Moan, moan, moan, moan for mile after dusty mile. I'd been on the road four days too, but you didn't hear me complain. Cactus, tough? Ha! Tough as a plate of yellow jelly! Sally

The greatest worry was that someone was watching every painful step. Our friend, Blue Jay.

'Give three hoots and see if he comes to help us,' Sally suggested.

'Some chance!' I snapped.

Sore feet bring out the worst of his prickly temper. Sally

My neck was burning, not so much from the midday sun as from the feeling that a pair of eyes was boring into it. At last I could stand it no more. I turned to the ridge that ran above us and gave three hoots. 'Tu-whoo, tu-whoo, tu-whoo!'

There was a soft thud of hooves and the tall Indian appeared on the crest of the ridge. 'Yes, my young friends? What can Blue Jay do for you?'

'I don't suppose you could find us a couple of horses, could you?' Sally asked.

Blue Jay's pony picked its way down the rocky slope to our path. The Indian slid to the ground. 'No...but you can take my pony, Swift Cloud,' he offered. 'She is strong enough for both of you. I will walk. You may leave the pony with my Flatfoot friends when you reach Fort Kearney.'

'Oh, but we're not going that far,' dumb Sally began. I didn't want this Flatfoot to know that we'd be going just as far as Ghost Town. I tried to kick her ankle – to warn her not to say too much. The trouble was, I missed Sally and kicked the pony instead.

The startled pony reared and Blue Jay gave me an odd look. 'There is an old Flatfoot saying,' he muttered with a shake of the head. 'Never kick a gift horse on the leg.'

He walked to the top of the ridge and waved as we trotted along the road. 'Don't go near Ghost Town!' he warned.

We waved back. 'We won't!' I cried. But half an hour later, we slid off the pony and found ourselves alone in...guess where!

15

The Treasure of Crazy Horse

Ghost Town had been small, even when it was alive. A saloon, a few stores, a blacksmith's shop and a livery stables. Just the sort of place for a stage coach halt.

Just the sort of place for a funeral if you ask me! Sally

A cold wind blew dust and tumbleweed down the main street. Doors creaked a sad tune on broken hinges. I was hoping we wouldn't have to spend the night in this dead place.

'Where do we start looking?' Sally asked.

I shrugged. This may sound stupid, but I'd been so worried about getting to Ghost Town, I hadn't thought about what we'd do once we *got* there.

He's right. It does sound stupid! Sally

'You know,' I said slowly, 'that's what the skinny Indian asked, back in the Dirty Shame Saloon. He said, "Where?" I remember now.'

'And what did the fat Indian answer?' Sally asked eagerly.

'Nothing. He just chuckled and said. "Well, well, well".'

'But he must have known!' Sally argued.

'Perhaps it's on the map,' I said. 'A cross marking the spot or something.' I pulled the map from my pocket and peered at it closely. I shook my head. 'Nothing!'

'But look at those letters,' Sally said quietly. 'The first letter of "Dirty Shame Saloon" is written in thicker print.'

I nodded. 'So is the first letter of "Old Cattle Trail". I wonder if that means anything?'

It did! I looked carefully at the map – especially the letters in thicker print – and I knew where the treasure of Crazy Horse was buried. Can you work it out? Look at the map and see. Sally

Of course, the bleach-blonde brain-box worked it out first. The first letters of **D**irty Shame Saloon, **O**ld Cattle Trail, Umbah **W**ater, **N**arrow Creek **W**ater, **E**xit, **L**onesome Prairie and **L**onesome Trail spell out D–O–W–N–W–E–L–L.

Down well!

The well was at the end of the weed-choked street, and we ran towards it.

'You go down in the bucket!' I called to Sally.

'*You* go down!' she yelled back. 'It's dark down there!'

When we reached the edge of the well, I explained. 'Look, you aren't strong enough to haul me up with all that treasure. But I should be able to manage a skinny kid like you.'

She sighed. 'I suppose so . . . if there really *is* a lot of treasure. How much do you think there'll be?'

'Oh, enough for both of us, I imagine,' I said vaguely.

'But what did the fat Indian with the map *say* about the treasure?' she insisted.

'Ah . . . he didn't exactly call it treasure – he used a Flatfoot word. It meant "precious things".'

Sally's cheeks glowed red with anger. ' "Precious things"!' she exploded. 'We've come all this way and faced death a dozen times just for Crazy Horse's precious things?'

'But Crazy Horse was a great Flatfoot chief . . . he fought against General Layton at

Deadwood River. He *must* have had a fortune.'

Sally's mouth was tight as a rat trap. She climbed over the well wall and eased herself into the bucket. Her blue eyes sparkled and her blonde hair bristled. 'Lower me down!' she ordered in a chilly voice.

I lowered the bucket steadily till Sally called for me to stop. A few moments later, my heart jumped into my mouth when I heard her yell. 'I've found it!' I wound the rope up quickly.

Sally stepped out, clutching a leather saddle-bag covered in dust and cobwebs. My hands were shaking too much to unfasten the buckles. Sally unfastened them. We pulled out the treasure of Crazy Horse...

16

The Spirit of Crazy Horse

We laid out the treasure of Crazy Horse on the wall of the well.

There was a tomahawk, a feathered head-dress, a bead necklace and a painting of a fierce Indian with the name 'Crazy Horse' above it.

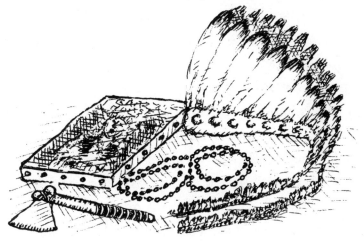

'Crazy Horse's treasure,' Sally murmured.

'Crazy Horse's precious things,' I sighed.

'Crazy Horse's precious things,' said a deep voice behind us. My hand flew to my gun and I pointed it towards the fat Indian who had crept up behind us. It was the Indian from the Dirty Shame Saloon. He quickly raised his hands in the air. He wasn't armed.

'How did you get here?' I asked.

He shrugged. 'That treacherous Indian in Sad Gulch stole my map – but I'd already read it and knew that the trail ended in Ghost Town. And the Flatfoot have been watching you ever since you crossed the Black River . . . They helped me get here before you. I've been watching you from that deserted store over there.'

'Why would the Flatfoot help you?' Sally demanded.

'Because I am Little Horse, son of Crazy Horse,' he said. 'And that is my father's treasure.'

'It *was* his treasure,' I sneered. 'It's ours now!'

Little Horse nodded. 'It is yours now,' he agreed. 'Unless you choose to give it to me.'

'Why should we do that?' Sally asked. 'The Flatfoot think that Crazy Horse is their greatest hero. They could rally round the treasure: that's what Mrs Layton reckons . . . Take it as a sign that they should go on the warpath again.'

Little Horse answered quietly. 'They *could*, but that is not the reason I want the treasure.'

'Then tell us,' Sally said.

The Indian sat on the low wall of the well and told us his story. 'My father died in North Dakota. His body was taken to the burial caves in Narrow Water Canyon,' he said.

I nodded. We'd been to that canyon on our way to Ghost Town, and met the old warrior – or at least met his skeleton, his restless spirit.

Little Horse went on. 'The funeral party was attacked by a band of Eighth Cavalry hoping to find some gold. They took that saddle-bag. A war party came to the rescue of the funeral party and chased the Cavalry through here. The soldiers hid the treasure here, hoping to come back for it later. The Flatfoot were too far behind to see exactly where.'

'So how did you know where to look?' Sally asked.

'One of the soldiers made a map – a map that went missing for many years, till I went into the Dirty Shame Saloon last week. And I won it in a poker game.'

'Finders keepers,' I shrugged. 'We got here first!'

Little Horse sighed. 'The treasure is not yours...'

'No, and it sure ain't yours,' I said.

To my surprise, he nodded. 'I agree. It is not mine.'

'Then whose is it?' Sally asked.

'It belongs to Crazy Horse,' the Indian said quietly.

'It's no use to him: he's dead,' I said coolly.

'His body is dead – but his spirit cannot rest. He cannot go to the Happy Hunting Grounds in the sky unless his precious things are buried with him. His head-dress – to show his power. His bead

65

necklace – to pay for his passage. His tomahawk —
to defend himself against evil spirits. So, I only ask
that you give me the treasure so that I can bury it in
the caves of Narrow Water Canyon.'

Sad story. I could see that Sally was almost
crying. But I was too tough for that . . .

Or too stupid. Sally

The way I looked at it was this. Those soldiers
must have seen something in there that was worth
money or they wouldn't have gone to all that
trouble to make a map. I'd worked hard to get this
treasure. I wanted to keep it and sell it.

*But could we sleep easy at night, knowing that the
spirit of poor Crazy Horse was still wandering those
burial caves? I wanted to hand it over to Little Horse.* Sally

There was only one person who'd been right all
the way along the line. I decided . . .

17

The Treasure of the Cactus Kid

'Go on, Cactus. Give him his father's treasure,' Sally said.

I looked at her. 'I'll do it...for you,' I said shyly.

Yes, I know I'm supposed to be tough – but even the toughest cowboy has a weak spot. I guess Sally is mine.

'And we'll do it for the spirit of Crazy Horse,' she added.

'You don't believe all that stuff about suffering spirits, do you?' I asked.

She shrugged. 'I don't know – but I do know that I'd never be happy thinking that it might be true. I don't want to lie in the dark and to hear the rattle of bones; to open my eyes and see the face of that Indian in the picture; to see his hands reach out towards me begging...Begging for me to free him from this world. What could I tell him when he asked me for his precious things?'

'I know what you mean,' I said. I turned to Little Horse. 'Well, I guess you win.' I handed him the saddle-bag with Crazy Horse's treasure in it.

The Indian smiled for the first time. 'And perhaps *you* win,' he said.

'How?' I asked. 'I have no money – I don't even have a horse.'

'But you have the friendship of Miss Sally – that is beyond price. And you have the friendship of the Flatfoot nation forever – that is worth more than gold,' he said.

That's true! Especially the bit about my priceless friendship! Sally

I sighed. 'But friendship won't buy me bacon, beans and coffee,' I moaned and shook my empty bag.

Little Horse frowned. 'Perhaps the Flatfoot can help their friends, Sally and Cactus,' he said. 'It is a long stage coach ride from Sad Gulch to Fort Kearney...'

'True,' I cut in, 'but I don't see how that fact helps us.'

'What those stage coaches need is a resting-point half way.' The Indian looked around. 'Just about here, in fact.'

'Yes,' I nodded. 'Ghost Town used to be a stage halt...until the Flatfoot drove the townsfolk out.'

'We drove them out because they were our enemies: they killed our buffalo and destroyed our land in their greedy quest for gold. But the Flatfoot would be glad to offer this town to their friends, Sally and Cactus,' he said.

I looked around the dismal and windswept street. But with my eyes half closed, I could almost picture it. Clear the weeds...Paint the saloon...Tidy up the livery stables...

Yes. This town could offer travellers food and drink...fresh horses...a blacksmith service. 'We could turn Ghost Town into a real gold mine!' I cried.

Sally nodded eagerly. 'It would be hard work though. Really tough.'

'That doesn't bother me,' I boasted. 'After all, I'm the toughest cowboy in the whole Wild, Wild West.'

She gave me a friendly punch on the arm. 'And the nicest!'

Well, it's true. Sally

'But you will need some money to get started,' Little Horse smiled. From the saddle-bag he took the picture of Crazy Horse. 'While I take my father's precious things to Narrow Water Creek, you can take this to Fort Kearney and sell it. You may be surprised at its worth...'

18

Ending and Beginning

And when we reached Fort Kearney, we found the money to start a new life in ten Ghost Towns!

I showed the picture to the commander of the fort; he snatched it from me. 'Why, this is worth a fortune!' he cried.

'A fortune just for a picture?'

'Why yes! Crazy Horse and his friend, Lone Eagle, are the two most famous Indians in United States history since they beat General Layton twenty years ago. Now, the camera became popular before Lone Eagle died: we have lots of pictures of him. But Crazy Horse died soon after the Deadwood River battle: no one has ever found a picture of him.'

'So, who wants one?' Sally asked.

'Newspapers, writers of books, museums ...
They'll all want to pay you thousands of dollars for
this picture!'

And he was right. In the end, we made five
thousand dollars at an auction. That bought us all
we needed to make Ghost Town the finest stage
stop in America...Except the first thing we
did was to change its name. Now we call it
Crazy Horse.

My *idea, naturally.* Sally

Of course it was hard work at first. But to our
surprise, dozens of Flatfoot braves came to help.
And it's been fun to see our efforts grow, day by
day.

The saloon will be opening soon and I know
we'll make a good living from it. Sally will play
cards just to keep the customers amused...

But I won't be cheating any more. Sally

...while I work in the blacksmith's shop – just
like Ma.

*But he won't be wrestling grizzly bears. Any time he
wants a fight, he can fight me!* Sally

71

We may make some sort of fortune from our adventure, after all. But we've already found the greatest treasure – and it isn't silver dollars or golden nuggets.

For the only treasure *really* worth finding is the treasure of true happiness. These are the riches which the treasure of Crazy Horse has brought us. When *you* discover that, then come to Sally – and I know what she'll say.

We told you so! Sally